Strains

of

Long Ago

~

B.A.L. McMillan

Formatting and cover design by Stephanie Flint

ISBN-13: 978-0-9895034-1-9

LiquidAmber Publishing

Henderson, Nevada

Dedication

To those who guard the secrets of a heart.

~

Strains of Long Ago

~

GALWAY, AWAKENED BY A STORM AND STILL SLEEPY, DREW back the curtain, noting his neighbor's kitchen light was on. Sometimes he thought Mrs. Dunbar never slept.

He showered and dressed quickly, then went downstairs and out onto the front porch. The rain had already stopped, but the air was misty. His newspaper, unwrapped, lay at the far end of the walk. The newspaper girl either did not have an arm or cared little about doing a good job. He didn't really mind. He liked moving into the mist, liked the deep green of wet Missouri mornings.

In his kitchen, he carefully unfolded the newspaper, grateful the first page was readable. A brief article caught his attention: A long-time resident, Harold Wilson, had been found dead in his storm cellar, ostensibly from a blow to the head suffered during a fall. Foul play was not suspected, though Wilson's wife, who found the body, informed police that some young men in the neighborhood had been causing problems. She didn't know why her husband had been in the cellar at night.

Galway expected Mrs. Dunbar to be at his back door any moment, because this was exactly the kind of news item she always noted—one that posited a mystery and allowed her to conjecture. His previous profession—attorney—had intensified her interest in crime, particularly murder. He could often answer questions about procedure or possibilities. He hadn't informed her, yet, that his short career as an attorney hadn't been enjoyable, though he was quite good at it. He preferred to work with his hands, to spend leisurely time with good people, and to allow his mind to wander. He wasn't lazy. He just wasn't talented or focused. At least, that was his self-assessment.

At 9:00, concerned that Mrs. Dunbar had not come bustling over as he expected, Galway crossed the wet, thick grass to her house. She answered his knock still dressed in her robe, her hair down, long, gray, with a curl that belied her age. She nudged the screen door open,

"Thought I'd check on you," he said, going inside.

Something was wrong. Her slate-blue eyes, usually bright with good humor and intelligence, regarded him dully.

"What's wrong Mrs. Dunbar? Are you ill?"

"Yes. Sick enough."

"Let me call your doctor." He headed for the mahogany half-table. The phone wasn't there.

"I'm just sick about people," Mrs. Dunbar said, suddenly tightening the belt of her robe and turning toward the kitchen. "Sick, sick, sick, sick."

* * *

He followed her. "Did something happen here last night? Did I miss something? Where's the phone?"

"Something happened, but not here." She opened a red-metal tea canister. "I put the phone in the closet," she said.

"Why?" Somehow this always happened. They talked in winding paths along the brain channels of Mrs. Dunbar.

"This'll take a few minutes to heat. Because if someone came in here at night, they could take the phone off the hook and I couldn't call out."

"But couldn't they just cut the wires outside anyhow, supposing they wanted to stop you from calling?"

3

"They might not think of it. But if they saw the phone, *then* they'd think of it."

"Okay. So what else is wrong?"

"Did you read the paper?"

"About the Wilson death? Yes. He was found in his storm cellar."

"I knew Harold Wilson. I doubt he fell down any steps. He was as light on his feet as a mockingbird."

"He was sixty-eight."

"I'm sixty-eight. I move pretty well."

"Yes, you do. What do you think happened?"

"I'm not sure, but I would *like* to be sure. Could you check it out next week, some day after the funeral? Otherwise, I might never know. The newspaper might not follow up. They like to jump onto something new all the time."

"I thought you knew the Wilsons."

"I used to know him. That was a long time ago."

"Oh." Galway thought he understood.

"I don't think *I* would fall," she said.

* * *

4

The Wilson neighborhood was pleasant, with wide, clean streets, green lawns, honeysuckle and hollyhock. Galway parked his truck six houses from the Wilsons', and began canvassing for work. He didn't need money, which was a blessing. He could indulge his desire to be a handyman and charge very modest fees. If he didn't do a job well, he didn't charge at all.

By the time he was on the long walk up to the Wilsons' two-story white house, his goal all along, he had been hired for one yard clean-up, one roof-patching, and one wasp-nest removal. The latter had him worried.

The Wilson porch was a tasteful gray, the paint unmarked by foot-traffic. Deep, roofed, shadowy, it swept around both sides of the house, a porch meant for social gatherings, lemonade, ice-cream, girls in white dresses, young men in dark trousers, white shirts, and loose ties.

When the door opened slightly and no more, he ventured, "Hello. I'm Galway Evans, I'm a handyman, and lining up some work in the ..."

The door was easing shut.

"The Parkers want a roof repair and the Davidsons have wasps ..."

She was still there.

"I'm a repairman," he said. "A handyman. I try to do good work."

In a moment, she pushed the door open, and stepped out. She was very tiny and so thin the flesh of her forearms was taut against the bones. The fingers of both hands slanted down and to the outside, rigid. Arthritis, he supposed, and painful.

"What's your name?" she asked.

"Galway Evans."

Her gaze swept the street. "Are you walking?"

"No." Galway smiled down at her, stepping back and trying not to be so very tall. "I parked my truck at the end of the block." He pointed. "That's it down there. The blue ..."

"I don't have anything today."

"That's fine. Tomorrow? Or later in the week? I can schedule ahead or come back. It's up to you."

She nodded absentmindedly, then stated in a slightly querulous voice, "I'll have some things to be packed up and taken away. Maybe you could do that?"

"I'd be pleased to. It's easy work."

A ghost of resentment touched her features, made him realize the irony in his statement. It was easy for *him*. He realized the packing must be of her husband's belongings.

"I didn't mean to be insensitive," he said.

Her expression acknowledged the apology. "I do need help. Could you . . . I have a storm cellar that isn't safe. I want it closed up."

"If you want it filled in or leveled, I probably can't handle it. I don't have a lot of equipment."

"Just board it up."

"That I can do. When would you like it done?"

"Tomorrow or the next day." She turned, lowering her stiff fingers toward the door handle.

Galway reached it first. "Let me," he said.

As he left, he peered down the Wilson yard. A shed directly behind the house blocked the deep backyard from sight, but a partly visible mound to the right was probably the storm cellar.

Galway felt guilty for having approached Mrs. Wilson at all. He, like Mrs. Dunbar, had an inquiring nature, but, also like Mrs. Dunbar, he thought kindness was the highest virtue. Mrs. Wilson was obviously distraught, and understandably so. He didn't want to worsen that.

A few houses down, his knock brought a couple to the door. The man was in a wheelchair, slightly behind and to one side of his wife, who talked to Galway through the screen door.

"I'm sorry," she said. "There's a lot of work, as you can see, but we can't afford any help just now. Maybe later."

Galway sensed the stress of the situation. They were a young couple, early thirties, perhaps. The wife was pretty, little rosebud lips, bright eyes, and very tense. So was the husband—his wife's words must have been painful to hear.

"I'll check back," Galway said. "I could fit your work in around some other jobs, and give you a special rate because it's filler work."

"Just leave a card." That was from the husband.

Galway did so.

* * *

"Well?" Mrs. Dunbar asked, calling from her back steps.

"I'll be there all next week, and will find out what I can."

She studied him, as if deciding whether to pursue the matter or not, then disappeared into the house. He wondered what project obsessed her now.

Galway sat on his own front porch till dusk fell. The air smelled sweet and fireflies gradually appeared, like a wink here, there, then everywhere. As a child, he had been frightened of them, but not for long. He missed his parents. Their death had freed him from their expectations and from their life style—his father and grandfather had been attorneys—but he would have stayed an attorney all his life rather than lose them. They were good people.

He went in the house once, to fix lemonade, but it didn't taste right. He needed a summer afternoon when he was sixteen, and set back in time, maybe in the 1800s, when young girls dressed up to sit on wide, sweeping porches.

Maybe he just needed real lemons. Or more sugar.

* * *

To fix a roof: have a ladder with solid hooks; wear tennis shoes; don't look down.

From somewhere in the neighborhood came music, faint but lovely. Puccini? Galway replaced bad shingles and generously applied sealant.

Later, he took the check from Mr. Parker.

"I hear there was a death in the Wilson family down the street."

"Yes. Harold Wilson. Fell down some stairs. You think you got all the leaks?"

"If I didn't, I'll come back, no charge. Just keep my card."

The man nodded, satisfied. "Not many people guarantee anything nowadays."

"I hear Mr. Wilson was a good man, but had trouble with some teenagers in the neighborhood."

"I don't know who that would be. But transients, yeah. They come from a shelter on Hawthorne. Some of them are real weirdoes."

"Have you had any problems?"

"No. I thought a guy was stealing my car one morning, but turned out he'd just rolled up the window. It *was* raining a little. He was a big bruiser."

"Do you know which ones Mr. Wilson might have . . ."

"I don't know about any of this and I've got to get back to my game. How come you want to know? Did you know Wilson?"

"No. Just talking. I have to deal with a wasp nest next door. I dread it."

"Just knock the nest down and run like crazy."

"Sure."

* * *

Supposedly the spray would reach ten feet, a puny distance, Galway decided, for an enraged wasp. The huge nest probably held thousands. Hoping no one watched, Galway drove his truck up the driveway. Leaving the door open, he walked halfway across the yard, slowly neared the nest, aimed the canister, and pushed the spray button. Even before the stream—ineffectively narrow and somewhat foamy—hit the nest, the wasps fanned out, seeking. How did they know what to look for? Standing still should be a good defense. He depressed the spray button a few seconds more, then ran to the truck, hopped in, and shut the door. Numerous wasps had followed and now looped outside the window. When some floated away, he crept out to spray the nest again and again dash to the truck. He out-waited the hardy ones and finally, with the nest mostly abandoned, he knocked it onto a sheet of plastic, quickly cocooned it, and tossed it in the back of his truck.

He felt a little ashamed at having deliberately batted down a creature's home, hard work, and future. On the other hand, he had added wasp-removal to his handyman experience. He washed his hands and rapped on the front door.

"Are they gone?" The lady of the house peeked toward

the tree, as if the wasps were watching. "You take the nest down, too?"

"Yes. And I checked the other trees."

"I'm just so afraid of those things. They hang around the spigot out there, and I can't use the hose. They buzz me."

"If you have a few stragglers, just call."

"You bet I will."

"I'm working for Mrs. Wilson this week. You know her?"

"Just to say hello. We go to the same church. She has a lovely voice, or used to. She sang in the choir."

"Someone said transients might have been involved in her husband's death."

"Really? They trail by here every day. There's this one guy, the way he walks, it's scary."

A car pulled behind Galway's truck, honked two quick blasts.

"My son." She waved him to back up. He honked again.

"I'll get out of his way. I appreciate the work." Galway started to leave, paused. "Is Mrs. Wilson easy to get along with? She's got a lot of little odd jobs lined up."

"I imagine she's fine. She doesn't mix much."

Galway nodded, smiled, and the woman smiled back. Her son was revving the motor. Galway eased the truck out more slowly than necessary, and smiled at the boy, too.

So there really was a teenager in the Wilsons' neighborhood.

* * *

Galway had mown and weeded the corner yard when he spied the man Mrs. Davidson might have meant. The fellow was wiry, with narrow shoulders, even narrower hips, and he minced—short, tight steps, his legs and feet close together, shoulders twisting with each step.

"Hey," Galway called, and sprinted across the street. The man had stopped, withdrawing a little. He held a cigarette between his thumb and index finger, brought it up and puffed quickly. Galway extended his hand. "Galway Evans."

The slight man transferred the cigarette, accepted Galway's hand briefly, looking away as he did so.

"I was wondering," Galway said, "if you were the gentleman who talked with Mr. Wilson over there." He gestured toward the Wilson house.

The man shook his head, puffed the cigarette again.

"Do you know who it might have been?"

Another head shake.

"It's very important."

The man glanced up slyly, not meeting Galway's eyes. "Billy talked to him."

"Is Billy around here?"

"No."

"Could you take me to him?"

"He'll be by."

"By here?"

Nod.

"What's he look like?"

Shrug. He minced away. He partly turned and spoke toward Galway's feet. "Got a cigarette?"

"No."

He was off.

Galway drove a few houses down, parked slightly past the home of the young couple. He carried one of his toolboxes to their yard, began uprooting weeds and volunteer trees.

He wasn't aware the wife had come outside until he heard her voice.

"I told you we can't afford any help."

She was perhaps on her way to work, wearing a powder-blue dress, and low, white shoes.

"There's no charge. I'm waiting until time to begin some work nearby. I thought you wouldn't mind if I did a few things around here. It's good advertising."

She had dark, curly hair, cut short, and dark blue eyes— delft blue, Mrs. Dunbar would say.

"Thanks," she said, after a moment.

"Sure." Galway turned toward his toolbox. "You have a good day."

She drove off and Galway trimmed along the wooden ramp. It needed repair. He was getting a drill and screws when he heard the door open, the hum of the wheelchair.

"I thought my wife told you we didn't need any help."

"She did. I just thought since I was waiting for the next job . . . " Galway offered his hand. "I didn't mean to insult you. Galway Evans."

The handshake was quite strong. "Phil Harper."

His face was square, with high cheekbones, deep-set, kind eyes, and a nice, quick smile. "Thanks," he said.

Phil Harper guided Galway to the back, showed him an unsightly junk pile. Galway loaded his wheelbarrow with the smaller stuff and carried the larger pieces one at a time.

"I appreciate it," Phil Harper said. "Can I get you some coffee? Maybe some eggs? I can still cook."

Galway accepted the coffee, waiting on the porch till Phil Harper hummed through the door again, a tray balanced lengthways on his thighs. Then they sat and talked.

* * *

"There are a number of boxes in the shed in the back yard," Mrs. Wilson said.

They stood in a small room just off the kitchen. Records filled all the bookshelves, except for the space taken by the stereo and a few music books. A port-colored guitar rested in a stand in one corner; in another, a banjo, dark gold pegs around the drum, ivory inlay up the neck. A stool in front of the stereo suggested Mr. Wilson had sat here to listen to his albums and perhaps to play along.

"These instruments are worth quite a bit of money, Mrs. Wilson. You shouldn't just throw them away."

"Please give them to someone," she said. "Or take them yourself."

"Are you sure? You might change your mind."

"No." Her eyes flicked over the room. "No, I won't." She retreated into the kitchen..

Galway sat on the stool and lifted the guitar. It had been

played often, by a strong hand. The wood between the first three frets was worn dull, almost imperceptibly grooved. The strings across the sound-hole were bright. The banjo appeared equally enjoyed. He flipped through the albums— all folk music, bluegrass, blues, old-time.

"Are you ready?" She had come to the doorway.

"Yes. Sorry. I got involved in the instruments. I don't play, but I like this kind of music. All music, actually."

"Most people do," she said.

He was to box up everything in this room and in Mr. Wilson's bedroom upstairs, the south bedroom with the blue rug. She led him through the kitchen to the back door, and walked onto the back sweep of the gray porch, and indicated the shed. Her hands were too twisted to point. "It's unlocked," she said, and left him.

Galway walked to the shed. About fifteen feet farther down was the storm cellar mound, its top mostly dirt and straggly grass roots. A little terracing would allow the grass to take. He walked around it. The rippled-aluminum door slanted enough to guide rain down the slope of the yard. A pecan tree and apple tree obviously benefited from the runoff.

Since he hadn't been told to clean the cellar, he had no

excuse to examine the interior. Galway turned reluctantly to the shed. It was neat, the empty boxes stacked by sizes on a wide shelf along the back. He carried some to the house and upstairs. In Mr. Wilson's bedroom he folded suits, vests, cotton shirts, robe, jeans, flannel shirts, sweat suits, packed dress shoes, boots, galoshes, wading boots, and tennis shoes. Probably he would have liked Mr. Wilson.

Music suddenly swelled from somewhere downstairs—a violin, the sound deep and sweet, then faster, lighter, higher, like a change of seasons, rain. Joy. The volume softened, turned down by his employer, Galway supposed, though he could still hear it well. He listened for a short time before concentrating on his work.

He was loading the first boxes when he glanced out the window and saw Billy—possibly Billy—walking from the west beside the man Galway had spoken with earlier. They each carried and sipped from large paper cups. Galway hurried down the stairs, past the parlor, onto the porch. "Hey," he yelled, and again sprinted across the street.

He learned that in Billy's forthright opinion, the guy who died could really play that banjo.

"Harold Wilson," Galway offered.

"Yes. Mr. Wilson. He didn't have to look at the strings.

His fingers just peppered along. Any song."

Peppered.

* * *

Later, Galway reported on the day's events to Mrs. Dunbar and showed her the instruments he had brought home. "I can understand her giving them away," he said, "but not so soon. They're really good instruments. The guitar's an old Martin, the banjo a Star. Together they're worth about four thousand dollars, at least. Actually, you can't put a price on a good instrument."

"Maybe she doesn't know what they're worth. William had a guitar once, and only paid twelve-and-a-half dollars for it. At Sears."

William was Mrs. Dunbar's husband, deceased. Galway already knew a lot about him—he had been "a better man than will come again."

"I suspect Mrs. Wilson knows their value," Galway said. "She just wants them out of the house. Maybe that's normal in these circumstances. She's grieving."

"She should be. Do you think he fell down the steps?"

"I don't know. Something's wrong. According to the

news article, she said young men in the neighborhood had caused problems. So far, there's only one young guy, and no one has mentioned problems. There are *transients*. Maybe she just got rattled or is an imprecise person."

"Do you mean old? Some people, you know, stay sharp and spry until the day they die. Harold Wilson was a nimble man."

"He could have been ill, Mrs. Dunbar, on medication."

"Older people aren't always sick, or on medication. And he wasn't old. He was my age."

She left, a little huffy. He watched her cross the yard, turn down by the side of her house and then reappear, going inside for her evening ritual of turning on lights, bolting doors and checking closets. He wondered what project she had underway. He stretched out on the sofa.

The evening light fell across the bookcase, catching the deep colors of the instruments. The Martin was beautiful, a D28 in loving shape. He had probably grossly underrated its value. The banjo had one scrape near the tail-piece and one dent on the back of the neck. On the dark fret-wood were bits of a fine powder. He got up, bent down to examine the substance, and blew lightly. Most of the white still clung. He lay down again. The banjo had been Harold's main instrument—most of his albums were of banjo artists. No classical music had been in the small room off the kitchen. Mrs. Wilson must keep her music somewhere else.

The instruments darkened as night descended.

Galway woke in a moonlighted room. He groaned, sat up. His body wanted to work, but his muscles were lazy. He headed for the staircase, then remembered Mrs. Dunbar's odd trip down her side yard. He took the flashlight from the kitchen drawer and walked barefoot outside and to her house. He flicked the light along the wall and saw it immediately. She had painted the telephone wiring white to match the house. She was still thwarting imaginary burglars.

* * *

"You ever talk with Harold Wilson?" Galway asked Phil Harper the next day.

"Some. If I was outside when he passed by, we'd have a few words. He had served in the Army, too."

"Did he ever talk about his home life? Anything personal?"

"Not really. I knew they didn't have any kids."

"I hear he was quite a musician."

"Apparently they both were. He said he taught himself,

from records, and used to travel around to festivals. He said I could learn if I wanted—it was never too late to start."

"Do you play?"

"No. Oh, I used to fool around with a guitar some, in the service. It belonged to a buddy. When he got transferred, I stopped. Played a little blues."

"Blues—every man's music at some time in his life."

Phil laughed, not a real happy sound. "Yeah."

"Did you ever hear the Wilsons play?"

"Sort of. We could hear the banjo. I guess he would have been outside then, maybe on the porch."

"So he played alone?"

"I think so." He tilted his well-shaped head. "I probably would've noticed another instrument."

Galway stopped by the Davidson house, where he found a few wasps floating around, trying to find a home they had left the day before and lost forever.

"I can handle a few," Mrs. Davidson said, "but if you want to kill those stragglers, it's okay with me."

He talked with her casually, about how pleasant the area was, the congenial neighbors, nicely manicured properties. Without real deceit or nosiness, he gleaned confirmation that this wasn't a neighborhood for young people or trouble.

"We pretty much leave each other in peace," she said.

"I'm still working at the Wilson place," Galway said. "She's a little distressed now."

"Of course she is."

"I know her husband was a good musician. You said she used to sing?"

"Yes. But she has that terrible arthritis, you know? The real crippling kind." She shuddered. "Lord, I would hate to get that. And then she started losing her hearing. I don't know if the two are related, but they might be. I mean, often one illness leads to another."

* * *

"I hate to just board up the cellar door, Mrs. Wilson. The wood might be an eyesore. I could brace the aluminum door itself and nail it shut. That would keep kids out, just in case, but it would still look like what it's supposed to be, a storm cellar. I could also cover the mound with sod from the back of your lot and get grass growing again. It wouldn't look bad. I can't level it for you."

"Just seal it, Mr. Evans, the fastest way." She was dressed in black today. Her skin was translucent over delicate bones.

She had been lovely, he supposed. Still was, Mrs. Dunbar would say. Fairy-like. "You like Puccini, Mrs. Wilson?"

"Among others. He's always been a favorite."

"Did Mr. Wilson like opera, too?"

Her pale blue eyes looked stricken, only for a moment. "Yes, he did. Not as much as I. His taste in music . . . He liked everything. He was an active man."

"I hear good things about him."

This seemed to surprise her.

"From people in the neighborhood," Galway explained. "They've expressed regret."

"Cover the cellar anyway you choose. It really doesn't matter."

"Should I box up anything down there?"

"No. There's nothing of value."

"And there's no reason to keep it open for a while longer?" He spoke very gently, as if the question could harm her.

She responded matter-of-factly. "The police took pictures. I called the morning after talking with you and asked if I could seal it up. An officer phoned back and said yes."

"Then I'll start the job now and get it finished as quickly as I can."

She accompanied him to the sun porch, gestured toward

the cellar, a sloping, low mound to their right, perhaps thirty feet from the outside wall. "The shed is unlocked if you need anything. Or ask me. I'll be in the front."

"You don't want to check it out before I start?"

"No."

"I could bring up anything you want to save."

"It's being saved where it is. I don't want to make any decision."

"Right."

Moments later, standing before the cellar, he glanced toward the house. She was still in the rear room, her black dress fading into the shadows, leaving her face and hands ghostly and disembodied. Galway was sorry about this whole mess, though he didn't know what the whole mess was. He thought she was somehow trapped.

The cellar door was heavier than it looked. The outer handle was metal, long, set near the edge of one side, and below center. Leather under-hinges kept the door from opening fully flat and a long leather strap allowed it to be pulled shut by a person inside. The steps down were fairly steep, sparing the little space for shelves and a rough work table, the latter fashioned from sawhorses and a plywood panel.

No matter which way Mr. Wilson had fallen, he could have struck his head on something—a raw shelf edge, a sawhorse leg, a stack of unused bricks. Galway looked up at the opening. Or Wilson could have been struck by the door itself as he tried to close it. Galway flicked on a wall switch. A yellowish light seeped over the room. He turned it off, preferring the dimmer, natural light that filtered in.

The narrow shelves held old, empty Mason jars, stacked copies of *Old-time Banjo Magazine*. On another shelf lay a violin, neck broken, bridge down, strings dangling. Galway picked it up gingerly. A white dusting of rosin still clung to the black, fretless neck. The instrument was very old and had been repaired before its last disaster. A triangular patch the size of a thumbnail had been carefully glued back in place. Only on close examination, like this, would the patch be visible. The neck had been rejoined to the body once before, too. The last break had been final, though, grand scale, as if someone had swung the instrument against something solid or had stepped on it. He read the inscription inside the violin. It had been handmade by Thomas Carlton, 1892, Pennsylvania. This likely belonged to Mrs. Wilson. Galway didn't want to leave it here, but he had been told nothing of value was in the cellar. He wasn't ready to ask her about it, and certainly not ready to take it against her will. He placed it lengthwise on the center of the shelf. A small container of rosin lay nearby. He moved it closer to the violin.

He leafed through the magazines. They offered glimpses into another world that at least one of the Wilsons, maybe both, had experienced.

The door was constructed of one wide piece of corrugated aluminum mounted on a heavy wooden frame of cross boards. Galway drilled pilot holes, then connected the door and frame to the underframe with four-inch screws, sealing each puncture with silicon. The cellar was safely closed, but could be reopened without too much trouble. Once he cleared away the minor debris of his own handiwork, it looked as it had before. Then, taking Mrs. Wilson at her last and not first word—to cover the cellar as he chose—he transplanted sod to the cellar mound and watered it down.

Galway took the check from Mrs. Wilson. "Thank you," he said. "You don't have anything else you'd like done?"

"No. I can't think of anything."

Dusk was flowing into the room behind her, a large room with oak floors, dark, polished furniture.

"I went ahead and put sod over the cellar."

"I saw."

"I thought I'd come by late each day, water it for a week. That'll give it a good start."

"No. If it needs water, I'll do it. You needn't come back."

"I'll be in the neighborhood anyway. And I like to finish things right. There's no charge for a follow-up."

He took her silence as acquiescence. "You won't even know I'm here," he said.

As he left, fireflies were blinking everywhere in the Wilsons' yard. A late-day gathering. He smelled the damp soil and grass. Nostalgia for something filled him and he felt briefly deeply alone.

Galway wondered how Mr. Wilson's banjo, now in Galway's home, came to have rosin on the fret board. The banjo had been in the house; the rosin in the storm cellar.

* * *

"I can see how she closed the door," Galway told Mrs. Dunbar. "It's hinged not to open flat, so anyone could shut it—just give it a shove. But how could she open it? There's no latch, but I still didn't find it very easy to do."

"Maybe she didn't. Maybe the police did."

"She opened it first. I'm fairly sure of that. She took his banjo inside the house before the police came."

"How do you know?"

"I think he was playing out there, or meant to, and had the banjo with him. It had been banged up, probably recently, and there was rosin on it, not much—the rosin was in the cellar. The door could have hit him when it was shut. Or maybe he just dropped the banjo when he fell. All the little things have to add up."

"They eventually will. May take years." Mrs. Dunbar rose, took pencil and paper from a narrow drawer, and handed them to Galway. "Draw the outside scene for me, the cellar door and back yard. Give me an idea of the angles and space. It doesn't have to be art, just basically accurate."

He did so, roughly but quickly.

"How big are these trees?"

"They're shade trees. Maybe twenty feet tall."

"Could she have put a rope over a branch for leverage?"

"The trees are on the wrong side of the door. The pull would have to be from the hinged side, up and back. I doubt she could get a rope over a branch. She's neither strong nor agile, not anymore."

"I'm sorry." Mrs. Dunbar studied the sketch, and so did

Galway. Her intense scrutiny made him feel that perhaps he had drawn in the answer.

"You said that man down the street had a wheelchair?" she asked.

"Yes."

"Could she have borrowed it?"

"I don't think so," Galway said. "People don't loan wheelchairs. At least I don't think they do. Why?"

"She could have used the motorized chair to help her pull the door."

"Okay. But she'd have to know how to use the wheelchair, get it up to her place, and would have had to return it. And she'd probably have to fabricate a reason for it all. It seems unlikely. Too cold, too. Planned."

"That couldn't be the case?"

"I think not." He remembered Mrs. Wilson's delicate face, the stricken look in her eyes. "No. She's a nice lady, Mrs. Dunbar."

"Well, I suppose she would have to be."

* * *

The next day Galway downed a wasp nest for a family

named Meakin who had heard about his prowess, and he moved huge, flat stones from one of their flowerbeds to another.

Afterward, he watered the sealed storm cellar, and imagined Mrs. Wilson's tiny frame struggling with the cellar door. He also imagined she watched him. Before he left, he took an old broom from the shed and swept her front walk. He wanted her to feel a friendly presence around her house, though he wasn't sure how a person did that without talking.

On Friday, Galway began painting the Harper house, at no cost to the Harpers. "I paint well," he said, "and I'd like people to know it. This is advertising." As Galway turned back to his work, he saw a large man across the street. The fellow had a long full beard and a thick mane of unruly black hair, was dressed in black, shapeless pants and shirt. Galway leapt from the ladder, dropped the brush, and ran, calling, "Sir!"

The man waited. His skin was inordinately pale, as if he had been kept from the sun a long time, but something in the cast of his eyes assured Galway he was friendly and kindhearted. He didn't seem to mind Galway's questions, and answered easily.

"I did talk to the lady in that house, just a few days ago. Yes. She asked me to tie knots in a rope."

"What kind of rope?"

"Just a regular rope. It was soft. Cotton, I think, but strong enough." He glanced at his palms. "It wasn't twine."

"What kind of knots?" Galway asked. "I mean, what did she ask you to do? Specifically."

"She wanted me to make a loop at each end, a noose, really, that would slide easily. I asked her what she was doing, and she said she was roping off a garden."

"Did she ask you to tie it *to* anything?"

"No." He drew back. "She didn't try to kill herself, did she?"

"No."

"Well, that's good. I hadn't thought of that till now. But she wasn't a very happy woman. I mean, no one can really tell, but . . . Why are you asking me questions? What's happened?"

"I'm trying to help her."

The fellow nodded, hesitating to move on, as if Galway might have something else to say. Galway recognized the pause and quickly took out and proffered a five-dollar bill.

"Are you sure the lady is all right?" the man said.

"Yes."

He took the money with a gracious nod and soft "Thank you sir."

* * *

"It would be hard," Mrs. Dunbar said, "to lose the music, the playing of it."

"Yes, it would. Especially if your partner continued playing." Galway helped himself to another piece of chicken, wondering again how the skin could be both crisp and soft, a uniform gold all around. Mrs. Dunbar had prepared mashed potatoes, too, thick, white gravy, green beans, and had set out applesauce, sliced white bread, and butter.

"Well, I don't think she had anything to do with it," Mrs. Dunbar said.

"That's a change of attitude, isn't it?"

"No. I never said I suspected his wife *did* anything. I just didn't think he fell."

"She's lost more than just the playing of music," Galway said. "She's losing her hearing. She watches my lips when I talk, turns stereo volume way up, but keeps it bassy."

Mrs. Dunbar scooted three green beans around her otherwise empty plate. She speared one and ate it quietly. Then she got up, brought the teapot to the table, filled both their cups. "Sharp tones may hurt her ears. The body tries to compensate for loss, you know, and strains what does work."

"Really?"

Mrs. Galway nodded. "William's brother went deaf that way. He said tinny sounds were like needles. Later, when he was totally deaf, he heard noises *inside*, crashes and rattles and whistles. He used to jump, startled from inside. That would be an ugly life, wouldn't it? Something you couldn't turn off. No rest for the weary."

"She's weary all right, and I imagine she doesn't rest. She looks tortured. I'm sure she was in the cellar. She got the door open, she found him, and she brought in the banjo. But thinking isn't knowing."

"Be direct. Ask her."

"I'm thinking about it," Galway said. "How did you know Harold Wilson?"

"He was in my class. He used to have a crush on me. Or maybe I had one on him."

"An old beau. I knew it."

"No. We never dated. He was so lively, so funny and

agile. He once slid down a drainpipe at high school. We were in an upstairs room, the windows open with no screens, and he just got up and exited." She smiled, her blue eyes quick and happy. "That was grand," she said. "Just grand."

"I don't want her to have done anything wrong," Galway said.

"Maybe she didn't. But losing what you are is really difficult to accept, Galway. A person doesn't become a saint just by loving someone. Love can make a devil, too."

* * *

While the sun still climbed, Galway finished painting the Harper house, with Phil Harper at ease now, sitting in the shade, responding when Galway asked what patch needed another coat, and saying he was getting good at accounting, if Galway ever needed that kind of help. Then they ate hamburgers in the Harper kitchen and talked about the difficulty of doing work you didn't like. Galway loaded his truck, strolled to Mrs. Wilson's, where he watered the transplanted sod. He rolled up the hose, hooked it onto the ramp of the shed, and stood looking at the expanse of deep, well-cared-for lawn, now grown past neatness. He would mow it, but he had another purpose at the moment.

He opened the shed door. A rope, very loosely coiled, was in the corner to the right. He vaguely recalled seeing it earlier. Two large hooks on the wall above suggested it usually hung there. It was old, had obviously been well used. It was also quite long, and at each end was a loop, a slip knot as the bearded fellow had described. She could have pushed one end through the handle of the cellar door, and have slipped both nooses over the lawn mower handle. By leaning against the handle she could have moved the mower forward and thus lifted the cellar door. Shreds of dry grass were on the floor and on the rope. He assumed a mower usually sat where the rope now lay. He went outside, walked to the rear of the shed. Behind lush, fully-blossomed hollyhocks was a dark shape. He drew aside some branches. There was the mower, a medium-sized, old electric—its narrow cord still attached to a thicker, dark-green one that disappeared on the other side of the mower.

A bumblebee hummed close, and Galway stepped back. "All yours."

Galway went home for a while. Then he drove to the nearest library branch, and began a computer search for

Harold Wilson and bluegrass. After following numerous links across myriad modern channels, he found a second and third place won at Winfield and some black-and-white photos of a duet called High Grass. "Hot instrumentals and tight harmony." Harold and Mary Elizabeth Wilson. He couldn't see much but there they were. Together.

He drove to the Davidsons'. Mrs. Davidson was well pleased that no wasp had appeared at her spigot. "They got the idea," she said, "and just moved on."

"Good," Galway said. "The natural way to get rid of a pest is to discourage it from hanging around, but most people haven't got the patience."

"Actually, I'd rather spray them. Or have you do it." She smiled.

"I was wondering," Galway said, "about Mrs. Wilson. You mentioned that she has a lovely voice."

"Used to have. Well, maybe still does. A couple of times she kind of apologized for being flat, or something like that. I'm not sure what she said. It was just a . . . an acknowledgment that she wasn't singing as well as she used to."

"Where was Mr. Wilson? He didn't come to church?"

"Oh, he came. He was still in the choir. He was a really fine tenor."

Galway went home again, put Harold Wilson's instruments in the cab of his truck, and drove back to the Wilson house. He got the mower from behind the hollyhocks, plugged in the cord, and began mowing the lawn. Mrs. Wilson came outside and stood by the shed, her thin arms folded at her waist. When he was raking up the grass, she left for a while, reappeared with a glass of iced water held between her two hands. He took it from her gratefully.

"This is a bigger yard than it looks," he said.

"Harold used to mow it in stages. Half in early morning, half in early evening."

"He was a very organized fellow."

"Yes, he was. He liked to stay busy."

He wondered how she kept her nails trimmed and buffed when her hands were so twisted. He assumed she went out for a manicure, but then she was capable of enduring pain without protesting much. He gathered that, at least, and he trusted his assessment. Her luminous, sad eyes were his evidence.

When she took the glass from him, again using both hands, he turned away. She could probably manage to do most anything. He finished his work, enjoying the labor itself, the sun, the smell of cut grass, and the near completion of his own goals. He put the mower and cord in the shed where they belonged, but gathered up the rope and tossed it into the back of his truck. Maybe he would burn it. He rinsed and rubbed his hands under the spigot and cupped water to splash over his face and hair. He smoothed down his hair as best he could and dried his hands against his jeans. Then, sitting on the edge of the Wilsons' front porch, shaded by a sweetgum tree, he took the banjo from its case. He couldn't play the instrument, and it wasn't a favorite of his. He preferred violin, guitar, and mandolin, though he couldn't play those either.

Harold Wilson had played out here, while his wife listened. He had kept playing when she couldn't bear to listen. She had stayed inside. Galway wondered how Harold Wilson had felt, what he had thought. Probably felt guilty. Maybe playing in the storm cellar had been a form of penance. Or—and Galway hoped this was the case—protection of his wife's feelings.

Galway heard the front door opening and watched Mrs. Wilson emerge. She sat in the gray swing. She seemed even smaller there, with her hands in her lap.

"I think you want to talk with me," she said.

Galway scooted back, leaned up against the post so she

could see his entire face, especially his lips. He held the banjo lightly, almost in proper position but not touching the strings. "I thought I'd give the banjo and guitar to a couple down the street," Galway said. "Phil and Gladys Harper. They're having a rough go right now, and music might be just what they need. Is that all right with you? That I give the instruments to them?"

"That's fine."

"It would be okay for you to change your mind, Mrs. Wilson. I'd give them back. And I'd open the cellar in a flash if you said so."

She shook her head.

"There's a fiddle in the cellar, a good one. Someone had repaired it before and maybe it could be repaired again."

She didn't respond.

Galway was newly aware of many tiny sounds, a bird here, a katydid, a wind-chime. He knew she heard none of them and never would again. They were too light, too high and musical.

"I was hoping to talk with you, Mrs. Wilson, just briefly, with no threat to you. I wanted to learn what happened here. I thought you might tell me."

She had been watching him intently, but now looked

away, across the street, where a young boy pedaled his bike furiously down the walk, as if in a race. When he veered behind a white block house, gone from their sight, Mrs. Wilson remained silent a short time more. Galway noticed that the underside of the eaves were blue, probably the original color of the house. Something always got left undone.

"We never had children," Mrs. Wilson said, as if picking up an earlier conversation. "We were so happy with one another, and we thought music was all we needed. Besides, there was time to have children later. But time slips away. Like they say."

"I found a photo of the two of you. High Grass."

"Yes. We were pretty good. He played with some other groups, too, for contests and performances here and there. He could have played seven days a week, seven nights. He didn't get tired of it. I didn't either, really. It's consuming, utterly consuming. It's a rich life." She seemed to be correcting someone's false impression. "It's not all ego, not about being on stage all the time. And it's not drinking or using drugs. It's . . . sound and story. That's it. You sing with someone and there's a moment when the voices wrap around one another, or become one, and it won't happen again just like that, and you know it. You're not even voices just then. It's a beginning and end. The harmony is so beautiful you want to hold it still, forever. We could sing like that, and play like that. We could be joy and passion and hope—everything. At least for moments. Then," she raised her hands, "this started."

"I'm sorry," Galway said. "It's a terrible disease."

"It was . . . so fast. The doctors told me it usually ran its course in about twenty years. I don't know if that's true or still true. A disease with a life span long enough to ruin your own. Odd, isn't it?"

Galway knew she didn't expect a response.

"It didn't take twenty years for me," she said. "I was thirty-five when it began. In five years, it had stopped me cold. For a while, I kept Harold company. But I couldn't bear it. I just couldn't. So I waited at home. I never asked him to give up performing, but he did. He dropped out of the circuit and took a job at the post office. He occasionally traveled to festivals. I didn't go along. Then, a new challenge." She tilted her head slightly, smiled, but her eyes were bleak. "Deafness, a little at a time."

"And sound hurt you?"

She nodded. "I was supposed to protect myself. No loud

sounds, no harsh sounds. Sometimes he would play and I would hear ringing for hours afterward. I couldn't tell him that. It sounded like jealously. But I eventually told him. And Harold, trying to keep what he could with no cost to me, played farther and farther away."

"He moved his playing to the storm cellar."

She nodded.

"Which left you alone in a different way."

When she remained quiet, Galway said "I think I know what happened, and I would like to tell you, but I don't want you alarmed. Shall I tell you?"

"Please."

"I think you felt abandoned, first by music and then by him. And in a way, you were abandoned. You had no recourse, because you couldn't ask him to give it up. That would be like saying come suffer with me. You couldn't do that. When he went outside that last night, to the storm cellar, you followed him. You didn't mean him any harm. Maybe you just intended to join him or to tell him how you felt. He left the cellar door open, leaning back on its hinge. Then, accidentally or deliberately, you pushed it shut. Whatever the cause, it was at least a protest. He would know you were out there. He would know you were upset.

But he didn't respond. He didn't emerge. You thought he might still be playing the banjo, as if nothing had happened, simply ignoring your anger. Maybe you were accustomed to such a reaction from him. So you went inside the house, to wait it out. Hours passed. You fell asleep, waiting. When you woke in early morning, and he still wasn't in the house, you knew something was wrong. You had to get him out, but you couldn't lift the door. And you were afraid to ask someone. You tried putting a rope through the handle and pulling, but you still couldn't move it. You tried tying the rope to the mower, but you couldn't tie the knots."

There was no denial or protest in her eyes. She was assenting to his interpretation. Galway thought perhaps she was relieved to hear the truth surface without her having to speak it.

"Then you saw one of the transients approaching and you asked him to tie slip knots at each end of the rope. He did so. When he was gone, you pushed the rope through the door handle, up to the mower and slipped the loops over the handle. You started the mower, leaned your weight against it. It worked. You had lifted the storm cellar door. When you went down there, and saw where he had fallen, saw the head injury, you knew you had shut the door at the wrong time. He must have been coming up the stairs at that precise moment. You realized you had killed him. I don't know how long you stayed there, but it was a sorrowful time for you. You brought the banjo inside and called the police."

"I thought," Mrs. Wilson said, "maybe he had been returning to the house."

"He might have been."

"Then what I've done is even more unbearable."

"You didn't intend it. It was an accident."

"You believe that?"

"Of course. Anyone would. You just want to be guilty because you believe you're being punished for something and you don't understand what. You've had too much pain, Mrs. Wilson."

His gentleness was her undoing. Her lips were trembling and he saw tears brimming. He feared if she cried, she might not stop. He leaned forward to touch, very lightly, her fingertips. "I'm not going to say anything about it, Mrs. Wilson, and I don't think you should. If you do, it might raise questions and there'd have to be an investigation—all to prove what we already know. In my opinion, even a little more trouble would be too much. If you want to tell the authorities, I'll go with you. I've been an attorney in my past, and would be again, for you. But the authorities are satisfied it was an accident. And it truly was. An unfortunate, terrible accident."

"When I found him," she said, "when I finally got the door open, I knew. I tried to wake him up. I would have died myself, right then, to wake him up."

"I know that's true," Galway said.

"I brought the banjo inside. I put away the rope and mower and closed the cellar door. And then I phoned the police. I should have told them what happened. I was afraid. I thought I would go to jail, and I wanted to save myself."

"That's understandable. I'd feel the same."

She sighed. Galway thought it a loving sound, sad and lonely, for good reason.

Evening was deepening. Galway stood up. "I'm going to take the instruments on to the Harpers. I'll be around anytime you need me."

When he got in his truck, she had entered the dark house. He started the motor, drove forward slowly, looking down the side yard. He had planted a few strands of honeysuckle on the cellar mound. With a little luck and some attention, they might take hold. He liked honeysuckle. It smelled sweet but was very hardy.

Later, as Galway pulled into the alley behind his property, the late-setting sun highlighted Mrs. Dunbar on a ladder at the side of her house. She was banging away at a section of gutter. It fell clattering down just as he turned off his motor.

"Look what I figured out," she said. He joined her, helping her drag the piece to the other side of the house, lift it up. She guided him, but he saw immediately what she was doing. The guttering would fit neatly along the phone line. "After I nail that in place," she said, "let's see anybody cut the phone line without waking the neighborhood."

When he told her the full story, Mrs. Dunbar cried and shooed him home. He understood. He was glad to go. There, alone, he started a fire. No matter that it was still summer and warm. He needed a fire. He showered, put on his robe, and sat in the dark staring at the flames. He had wanted to ask Mrs. Wilson when the violin was broken and by whom. But there had been no opportunity. They had come to the moment for compassion and not curiosity. He thought he knew, anyhow.

Galway thought of the young fellow who had slid down a school drainpipe, of young women who wore white dresses and sat on verandas. Women only looked frail. Who knew what strengths they had? The flames were red, yellow, only a flicker of blue here and there. Perhaps it would rain.

ABOUT THE AUTHOR

B.A.L. McMillan is a Missouri writer originally from Gravel Hill, Missouri. She is a student of psychology, herbal medicine, folk lore, religion, animals, and of literature on the subjects of ghosts, witches, and angels. She writes traditional mysteries and fantasies.

www. balmcmillan.com

A novel, the debut of Galway Evans and Letitia Dunbar.

www.ingramcontent.com/pod-product-compliance
Lightning Source LLC
Chambersburg PA
CBHW020623120726
47905CB00003B/923